THURSDAY'S BLINK

Genevieve Sipperley

dizzyemupublishing.com

DIZZY EMU PUBLISHING
1714 N McCadden Place, Hollywood, Los Angeles 90028
dizzyemupublishing.com

Thursday's Blink
Genevieve Sipperley

First published in the United States
in 2022 by Dizzy Emu Publishing

1 3 5 7 9 10 8 6 4 2

dizzyemupublishing.com

THURSDAY'S BLINK

Genevieve Sipperley

Thursday's Blink

Written By

Genevieve Sipperley

gsipperley@yahoo.com

Fade In:

EXT. THE POST BAR - NIGHT

LUX (V.O.)
It was a moment that lasted from dusk till dawn. ...it was unlike any other.

SHEA WALLACE (28, male) sits alone in his car outside of a rundown bar. There are no other cars in the parking lot.

INT. THE POST - NIGHT

Shea sits at an end of the bar and sips a beer. The bar only has a few other PATRONS scattered through out play pool and watch a sports program. LUX STONE (27, female) walks in and sits two seats down from Shea. She flags down AL (60's, bartender, male, slower paced) with a wave.

LUX
Can I get a vodka cranberry?

AL
I.D. please.

Lux slides her card across the bar.

AL (CONT'D)
This says you have blue eyes, they look brown to me.

LUX
Contacts.

Al gives her card back and winks at her then goes to make her drink.

SHEA
I didn't get a wink.

LUX
You might not be his type.

SHEA
Well he doesn't know what he's missing then.

LUX
You're a guy with the goods?

SHEA
Eh just a guy, more or less.

Al slides Lux her drink.

AL
Want to start a tab?

LUX
Is there a minimum?

AL
Only here for a drink?

LUX
Not sure yet. I was kind of planning on figuring it out as I went.

AL
I'll start ya a tab.

Lux sips her drink and watches one of the televisions that plays a show about alligators. Shea is on his cell phone and doesn't really pay attention to much of anything.

LATER

Shea swigs back the rest of what is in his glass and pulls out his wallet.

LUX
Take it you didn't start a tab?

SHEA
Yeah, I was just swinging by for a drink.

AL
Four drinks ago. Having another?

SHEA
No, I think it's time I call it a night.

LUX
Have some place to be?

SHEA
Not particularly.

LUX
Then what's wrong with being here till you have somewhere else to be?

Al puts a glass on the bar.

AL

This one's on me.

SHEA

Looks like I'm staying... So what brings you to this abandoned neck of the woods?

Lux gets up and scoots down to the seat next to Shea.

LUX

I'm not sure. I went for a drive and just kept driving. I had some things on my mind and I thought a car ride with the windows down would bring some clarity.

SHEA

Did it?

LUX

It brought me here. I turned down the wrong dirt road and saw the sign for this bar. The flicker of the lights drew me in.

AL

That's my gimmick. People keep telling me to get that light fixed, but why would I? All the other bars have their lights fixed, it adds character.

LUX

Needless to say, here I am. What about you?

SHEA

I'm getting married in two days. The house is full of in-laws and people I've never met before. I needed the break.

LUX

Rightfully so. Is this a local hang out for you?

SHEA

First time actually.

Lux raises her glass to Shea.

LUX

Cheers.

They take a sip and both are silent for a moment.

LUX (CONT'D)
Game of pool?

SHEA
I'm not so great.

LUX
We're at a bar, you don't have to be good.

SHEA
I'm really just here to get away. Not really looking to talk or play games.

LUX
Fair enough.

Lux and Shea sit in silence. Shea sips his beer awkwardly.

LUX (CONT'D)
It's just that I've been crammed in the car for hours and my knees are killing me. I could go play by myself, but then I would look a little.... Really you would be doing me a huge favor.

Shea looks around the bar which is now empty.

LUX (CONT'D) (CONT'D)
And there is no one else to ask.

SHEA
I won't judge you if you played alone.

LUX
Thanks.

Lux repositions herself in her seat and watches tv. Both take a few awkward sips.

SHEA
One game.

Lux has an instant smile and hops out of her seat.

LUX
I'll rack.

INT. THE POST - POOL TABLE - MOMENTS LATER

Lux takes a shot and misses.

SHEA
It seems this might be a long game.

LUX
I never said I was any good.

SHEA
I see that.

LUX
Are there any sports you are good at?

SHEA
Pool isn't a sport.

LUX
Don't tell those people in polos on tv.

Shea misses another shot.

SHEA
Like bowling, is that a sport?

LUX
I've broken sweat bowling before.

Shea gives Lux a look.

LUX (CONT'D)
I was hungover and the a/c was out. Regardless, I still broke a sweat. It could qualify as a sport.

SHEA
If you want to talk about real sports, yes, I played them. Basketball, track, soccer...

Lux misses another shot.

LUX
Oh, so you were a Golden Boy, huh?

SHEA
Something like that.

LUX
Do you still play things?

SHEA
Things?

LUX
Sports.

SHEA
Not anymore.

LUX
Why did you quit?

SHEA
I didn't quit, my knee did.

Shea misses another shot.

LUX
And that was the end of your glory days?

SHEA
That it was.

LUX
Do you have an all time favorite moment from that era of your life?

Lux misses another shot. Shea sits back and picks up his drink. Shea blinks for a moment.

SHEA
All Cup Soccer Tour. I was 17, very good looking, and could run that field like I owned it. We were playing countries from all around the world. In a semi final game, it was us versus Brazil. We were losing ten to zero, an obvious blowout. BUT... second half on a breakaway, our right wing Lawrence crosses the ball and I run in for a side volley - GOAL! We had our moment, and it was spectacular. Not everyone gets moments and for those of us that do, no matter what, those moments always end.

LUX
Obviously.

SHEA
I know obviously, but it doesn't mean I don't miss it.

Shea shoots and makes a ball in.

LUX
Of course you do. You had a hot haircut and felt like. But you will always have that day, it's yours. Like you own it... dusk till dawn. It's etched in your soul for life.

Shea makes another shot.

SHEA
Glory days always end.

LUX
That's why we have memories.

Shea misses next shot.

SHEA
What about you, any glory days?

LUX
Nah, I wasn't much for athletics. I was one of those art students.

Lux makes a shot.

SHEA
Any good?

LUX
I was amazing, still am. I just don't follow that passion anymore.

Lux makes another shot.

SHEA
Why's that?

LUX
I have that great displeasure of bills that seems to take most of my income. I just don't ever seem to have time to do what I want anymore. I always try to plan those personal days, but they just never seem to happen.

Lux makes another shot.

SHEA
Why don't you make them happen?

LUX
If time would give me a twenty fifth hour in a day, maybe I could look into it.

Lux makes another shot.

SHEA
Did you just get good all a sudden?

LUX
I guess so.

SHEA
Seemingly.

LUX
When you were six, what did you dream of doing or becoming when you were older?

SHEA
When I was six? Who remembers that age?

LUX
Alright, earliest you remember then.

Lux makes another shot. The 8-ball is her final shot.

SHEA
When I was eight I wanted to be a paperboy and save up money to live abroad. I also wanted to win my gym relay races.

LUX
You do realize a paper route doesn't provide for a very high salary?

SHEA
I was eight.

Lux makes the 8-ball in.

LUX
I do believe you own us a round of shots.

SHEA
There was no bet placed.

LUX
Are you sure?

SHEA
Pretty sure.

LUX
Pretty sure isn't a sure, sure.

SHEA
Shark.

Lux smiles.

INT. THE POST - BAR - MOMENTS LATER

Lux and Shea cheers and take shots.

SHEA
No chaser?

LUX
I like my whiskey. So, marriage?

SHEA
What about it?

LUX
I don't know, big deal?

Shea nods.

SHEA
Yup.

LUX
Do you remember the first girl you ever liked?

SHEA
Melissa Miller, first grade. She wasn't in my class, but I saw her every recess. I couldn't wait until after lunch and then all the classes were allowed to go outside for hald an hour. She always sat at the top of the slides with her friends. I would act like I was
(MORE)

SHEA (CONT'D)
using the slide and always go up there. They were first graders though, young, and to them all boys had cooties.

LUX
That's 'cause they did.

SHEA
Anyways, she was beautiful, but that isn't why I liked her. I liked how she always had stickers and shared them with her friends. And how she would giggle during class and the teachers would start to yell at her, but then she would give her coy smile and always get out of trouble. She was sweet, and she was kind.

LUX
What happened?

SHEA
She moved away half way through second grade. I'm not sure where, Pennsylvania, Panama... something like that.

LUX
You do realize those are two completely different countries?

SHEA
They both begin with P. Whereever she is, she took the love of my young heart with her.

LUX
How endearing.

SHEA
It is. What about you? Did a grade school fling steal your heart?

LUX
No, I wasn't really into boys until junior high.

SHEA
Come on, everyone had a grade school crush.

LUX

No, I honestly didn't. I don't know why. I was a tomboy and-

SHEA

You were one of the guys, that's why.

LUX

That's not why.

SHEA

You saw them as friends and they saw you as just another boy to play kickball with.

LUX

I was a badass at kickball, thank you very much. But that's not why.

SHEA

Then?

LUX

My parents split when I was six and I was one of those kids that swore off love with a strict vow.

SHEA

So what changed?

LUX

A boy with a black leather jacket and sunglasses.

SHEA

How cliche.

LUX

He was gorgeous, and he rode a BMX bike. We sat next to each other in Spanish. It's no wonder I never picked up a second language, I was too busy swooning over Guy's hair as it gently fell in his face.

SHEA

Wait, his name was Guy?

LUX

Oh, for sure.

SHEA

Seems to fit.

LUX
Every girl would doodle his name in hearts on their binders. Then, he asked me to the Spring dance.

SHEA
Dances in junior high?

LUX
Yeah, they were lame as lame could be. Dancing with arms fully extended, the guy's arms on the waist and the girl's arms on the shoulders. You had to be a foot apart or one of the fifty teacher chaperones would come and break you apart. Guy asked me. We met at the gym doors and walked in together holding hands. Everyone, I mean everyone, turned their heads. I felt like royalty for a split second, and that I was the most popular girl in the entire school. And you know what? For that moment, I think I was. We sipped colas and only danced to the slow songs. My palms were so sweaty, I kept worrying that he would be grossed out by them, but, he didn't mention it. Then, the night ended. He rode his BMX bike home. My mom picked me up in her minivan, and that was that.

SHEA
You guys didn't go steady or hold hands or do whatever it is that preteens do?

LUX
Nope, that following week he was supposedly dating a high schooler. Our night was over.

SHEA
Did you get a good night kiss at least?

LUX
Nope. I did get a hug though, which everyone saw. It boosted my rep and status for the remainder of the year.

SHEA
Nice.

LUX
Yup, I was a princess, even if just for a night.

SHEA
Like Cinderella.

LUX
No, I was way cooler than Cinderella.

Shea's phone RINGS. He looks at it and ignores the call.

LUX (CONT'D)
Ignoring the wife already?

SHEA
No, It's my mom. She and my fiance have been joined at the hip planning for the past six months.

LUX
Extra help must be nice.

SHEA
It is.

LUX
Then what?

Shea takes a long drink and then looks at Lux.

LUX (CONT'D)
Too personal? Did we cross that line?

SHEA
We just met.

LUX
Yes. But we met on accident.

SHEA
Accident?

LUX
Convenience brought you here, and a flickering light brought me here. That's not intended change or random, more of an accident.

Shea stares at Lux for a long minute and then LAUGHS.

LUX (CONT'D)
What?

SHEA
You are different, I'll give you that.

LUX
At the risk of sounding too different, do you want to grab a booth? These stools aren't the most comfortable.

SHEA
For the sake of comfort.

INT. THE POST - BOOTH - MINUTES LATER

Lux and Shea sit across from each other. Al brings them a round of drinks.

AL
For my best customers of the night.

Shea and Lux look around, the bar is empty.

AL (CONT'D)
There were other people in here before you.

Al walks away.

LUX
Two more drinks and two more shots, you won't get in trouble will you?

SHEA
I'm not on a leash.

LUX
I didn't mean it that way. You just seem like you aren't keen being in the midst of a wedding right now.

Lux can tell she hit a nerve.

Lux slides Shea a shot and then lifts hers.

LUX (CONT'D)
To you.

SHEA
I don't need a toast.

LUX
Well, you are getting one anyway.

Lux and Shea toast.

Lux sets up her empty shot glass and pulls a coin out of her pocket. She tries to bounce the coin in her glass.

SHEA
Do you like to play games?

Lux stops.

LUX
I like to keep forward momentum and never be stuck in a course of tension.

SHEA
What does that mean? You don't like conflict or that you don't like silence?

LUX
Neither I guess.

SHEA
Why is that?

LUX
Well, do you?

SHEA
I asked you first.

LUX
Indifferent.

SHEA
I doubt that.

Lux sips her drink.

LUX
Alright. Conflict, it's a useless ploy.

SHEA
Ploy?

LUX
I believe everyone is made with their own core entities and perception is an aspect that can be altered, but ultimately never changed.

SHEA
People change their minds all the time.

LUX
They change their decisions, but that doesn't mean they changed their perception. All that happened was that their perception was altered by an influence beyond themselves, or caused by themselves. How they, or we, see the situations is through the same eyes we've always had- the same frame of mind.

Shea tries to follow what Lux says, Lux can tell he might be confused.

LUX (CONT'D)
Say you paint the color yellow on a piece of paper, and someone convinced you it was too bright? Or that it needed to be orange? If you believe it is too bright, or that it should be orange because other opinions influenced or made you realize that- what do you do?

SHEA
I don't know, I'm not an artist.

LUX
My point being, you either leave it yellow, darken the yellow, add some red, or just trash the whole thing all together.

SHEA
Ok?

LUX
But that doesn't detract from the fact that the yellow, my original perception or thought will always
(MORE)

LUX (CONT'D)
be the basis of what follows. Conflict is avoidable if you are willing to alter your perception when needed, or voice your thoughts if you can anticipate the results.

SHEA
Do your friends like you?

LUX
They love me.

SHEA
And silence?

LUX
It hates me.

Shea taps Lux's glass with his and they both drink.

SHEA
Can I ask about your family?

LUX
Nothing much to answer. Mom and Dad split, I went with Dad, he raised me. No siblings or grandparents.

SHEA
I'm sorry.

LUX
Why?

SHEA
I have a really big family, and as annoying as it is, I would hate to not have anyone of them.

LUX
My dad is great! I never really needed anyone but him. He worked hard, made good money, went prom dress shopping with me-

SHEA
Wait, you went to prom?

LUX
And I was prom queen, but that story would only digress this one.

SHEA
Fair enough, continue.

LUX
Basically, my dad was a mom and a dad and he was so good a it that I never missed anything or thought I lacked another parental figure.

SHEA
What about birthdays and holidays?

LUX
Oh, my Dad was the best. European trips, practical presents, a family dog.

SHEA
You like dogs?

LUX
Dogs and cats, and turtles, and just about every living animal. My Dad drew the line though when I wanted a sloth and an octopus.

SHEA
The sloth I can understand, but why not a baby octopus? There are small ones that can fit in tanks.

LUX
Yeah, by octopus I mean like big ones and I wanted it to live in our pool out back.

SHEA
Ah, I can see why he may have said no to that.

LUX
Yeah, well, everyone has lines.

Lux and Shea sip on their drinks.

MOMENTS LATER

Shea's cell phone RINGS. He looks at the call screen and ignores the call.

LUX (CONT'D)
Mom again?

SHEA
Nope, Dad this time.

LUX
I don't mean to pry-

SHEA
Yes you do.

LUX
Yes I do... but why not just answer and let them know where you are?

SHEA
Because I don't know where I am.

LUX
Oh, I'm going to need another drink for this one.

Shea LAUGHS.

SHEA
I only mean that I'm not sure what to tell them.

LUX
About?

SHEA
The sum of it is, I'm having doubts about the wedding.

LUX
Well that's obvious.

SHEA
I'm not having doubts about my fiancee or wanting to be with her, it's more that we have been together for so long that getting married is the only next step. But what happens next? What is the next, next step? Do I have to have a kid and I'm going to be a soccer coach and drive a minivan, I can't drive a minivan.

LUX
Good news on that, they make some super stylish family cars these days.

SHEA
The minivan is just a metaphor. I just want things to be how they are now without the pressure of everything that is involved with marriage.

LUX
Yeah, you are kind of locked in after the I'Do's.

SHEA
And I just wanted space to think and really be able to say those I'Do's with all my heart and commit fully and I just wanted a second to myself in the midst of all the planning and pre-wedding chaos, so I took a drive. I was gone not even a half hour and my phone was ringing off the hook. Everyone thinks I am getting cold feet, and it's not that, I just wanted a second to breathe. Now I have to explain it more than that and I just don't have it in me right now.

Lux stares at Shea with no response.

SHEA (CONT'D)
You pick now to be silent?

LUX
There is a fire-pit out back I want to check out before he closes the patio for the night, care to join me?

SHEA
That is your response?

LUX
I understand your reasoning and I agree with you that maybe you just need some silence to catch a breath. I mean, I'll keep talking, eventually, of course.

SHEA
Is this your way of getting out of having to tell me about prom?

LUX
There isn't much to even say about prom. It's all so cliche. I was popular, there was a vote, I got a crown. All seems like a story now and I'm definitely not that same person I was in high school.

SHEA
You aren't the most popular anymore with a ton of friends on the cheer leading squad?

LUX
Well, I am most of that, but with a different way of approaching it. You probably get it, it's hard to believe that your weren't Mr. Popular!

SHEA
I was known, but I wasn't prom royalty or anything like that.

LUX
What about your sports?

SHEA
Among the ones I already told you about, I was the captain of the football team.

LUX
There it is!

SHEA
My school was small, so it wasn't a big deal.

LUX
Yeah, but come on, you know that is a big deal kind of thing.

SHEA
I just spouted about my wedding worries and you care about my high school popularity status?

LUX
No, I wasn't digressing. I think the way you feel right now is like me in high school - cliche.

SHEA
That's a bit harsh.

LUX
No, think about it. You have the kind of worries that come up on an internet search engine.

Shea appears to get frustrated.

LUX (CONT'D)
No, this is suppose to be a soothing thing. You have the doubts and fears as every other guy, and probably most all of those guys went through with it and got happily married. You don't want to change diapers and be uncool, you aren't ready to give up, in a very lose metaphoric sense, being the captain of the football team.

Shea leans back and nods his head.

SHEA
That actually does make sense.

LUX
Of course it does, it's my personal wisdom.

SHEA
I wouldn't use the word wisdom- perceptive at best.

LUX
I'll take that too.

SHEA
So I take it you dated the quarterback in high school?

LUX
I was the head cheerleader, of course I did.

SHEA
At least you are good with modesty.

LUX
Like I said, I'm not that person anymore. That doesn't mean I can't brag or be proud of who I was.
(MORE)

LUX (CONT'D)
Plus, I was one of those nice popular people not a mean girl.

SHEA
Not even a little?

LUX
Not even when I was on my period.

SHEA
Alright. What were you saying a few minutes ago about an outside?

Lux gets out of the booth.

LUX
There it is again, another search engine cliche: guys and their fear of the scary period.

Shea gets out of the booth.

SHEA
This round is on your tab.

Shea and Lux head to the bar.

INT. THE POST - BAR - MOMENTS LATER

Lux moves a few stools and stands at the bar.

AL
Another round?

LUX
If you would, please.

AL
(to Shea)
You as well?

SHEA
One more. And a glass of water.

AL
The classic one more order.

SHEA
This one really is my last one, I have to get back at some point.

LUX
Or it's late enough that you just need to get back by morning light.

Al gives them their drinks along with two shots.

SHEA
We do have to drive at some point.

Al pores them a glass of water.

EXT. THE POST - PATIO - MINUTES LATER

The outside is decorated like the interior of a post office.

Lux and Shea find themselves a seat next to a fire pit that has a decent size blaze. Lux props her feet up on the side of the fire pit.

LUX
Well this is cozy. Why have we been inside this whole time?

Shea doesn't make himself as comfortable.

SHEA
Seems like a waste of a lit fire when there is no one even in the bar.

LUX
We're here, isn't that full enough?

SHEA
It's not full at all, look at all of the empty space.

LUX
That's just more space for us to stretch out.

Shea doesn't respond to a coy smile Lux gives and instead takes a drink of beer.

SHEA
So what do you do for a living?

LUX
Nothing right now, kind of in between things.

SHEA
Is that why you are on the road and don't really have anywhere to be?

LUX
Who said I didn't have anywhere to be?

SHEA
I got a sense.

LUX
What if I did have somewhere to be, would you find me more interesting?

SHEA
Where you are or aren't intended to be doesn't make any difference to me. I am enjoying drinks right now.

LUX
Because we probably won't ever see each other or talk after tonight.

SHEA
Probably not.

LUX
What if we did, then would it matter what I was doing?

SHEA
But we probably won't.

LUX
Just what if?

Shea takes a minute before he responds.

SHEA
What if we talked past tonight? Would what you did, or do, or where you are, or aren't, on your way to matter?

LUX
Yup.

SHEA
I don't know, I guess it makes me think a little differently about how I would perceive you.

LUX
Like you wouldn't be talking with me right now?

SHEA
No. Like I would retain more-

LUX
So you would actually listen?

SHEA
No, not like that. Alright, so if we did speak again it would in a way be a follow up to this conversation. I would probably asked how you've been, if you ever made it to where you were going, what you were up to, and so on. All of the usual thought patterns. But because we have no future, there's more freedom in what avenues of conversation topics we can explore.

LUX
We don't have to talk about the real stuff.

SHEA
We're just talking and to be honest, it's been really nice to just talk.

LUX
I know what you mean. Our conversation doesn't have to have a purpose, a conclusion, a plot, a tone, an intention - the words just flow.

SHEA
Yeah.

There is a long pause.

Shea and Lux drink their beers and watch the flames.

SHEA (CONT'D)
Alright, what if there was a castle twenty feet from here and
(MORE)

SHEA (CONT'D)
heavily guarded by dwarves with nine foot arms covered in needles?

LUX
(Laughs)
What?

SHEA
It's my turn to ask a what if.

LUX
Alright, I would, let's see. I'd take the castle!

SHEA
And just how would you do that?

LUX
Simple. Finish this beer, break it and then sneak up behind one of the dwarves, snap his neck then slice him open and use his body as a suit to go right in the front door and go to town on anyone that stands in my way.

Shea stares at Lux with a shocked face.

SHEA
Wow.

LUX
Pretty good, huh?

Lux sits back in her chair satisfied with her answer and takes a drink.

SHEA
I'd say so.

LUX
You would do the same?

SHEA
I would just take pictures or something. I never said the castle needed to be taken.

LUX
Why else would it be there?

SHEA
In fictitious world, I have no idea.

LUX
In the real world?

SHEA
Oh man, I don't even know. Government experiment gone wrong?

LUX
A government fall back is way too easy.

SHEA
But sometimes so true.

A few beats pass.

LUX
What if your fiancee isn't mad at you for being out all night?

SHEA
I'd consider myself lucky? But believe me, she is going to care.

LUX
I know it's not my place to say, but out of all your missed calls, none of the calls were from her.

SHEA
She's kind of wrapped up in the planning and we agreed that we wouldn't see each other until the wedding.

LUX
Isn't that usually just for the day before?

SHEA
Or the week before.

LUX
Well, whatever the case of seeing each other, are you guys not calling or texting?

SHEA
We are.

LUX
I see that.

SHEA
That is an awful what if question by the way, mine had a lot more creativity and entertainment value behind it.

LUX
Uh huh.

LOUD NOISES from inside can be heard. GLASS BREAKS.

Lux and Shea look at each other and slowly get up and walk toward the door, Shea tries to lead but Lux pushes forward.

SHEA
(whispers)
Stay back.

LUX
You stay back.

SHEA
Shhhh.

Shea and Lux get to the doorway and look in.

INT. THE POST - CONTINUOUS

DON (older guy, flannel shirt) throws a stool as Al tries to calm the guy down but keeps his distance.

AL
Just have a seat.

Don picks up a candle off a table and chucks it across the room.

EXT. THE POST - PATIO - CONTINUOUS

Shea pulls Lux back.

SHEA
You wait here, I'm going to go help Al.

LUX
Or you wait here and I'll go help.

SHEA
Fine, how about we both go try to help?

Lux doesn't respond and proceeds inside. Shea takes a breath and quickly follows.

INT. THE POST - CONTINUOUS

Lux is crouched down as she scurries in.

Shea is a little more reserved as he crawls behind the bar.

Don now has a pool stick in his hand and smacks it over the pool table. Lux goes towards Don, but Don turns around and stops her.

DON
Who is this?

AL
A customer, don't pay her any mind and especially no harm.

Don lowers the pool stick.

DON
'Bout time you got a customer in here.

AL
I know, I know. Now will you grab your seat?

Shea pops up from behind the bar.

DON
Two customers?
(Laughs)
Man, you got yourself an old fashioned business now.

Don staggers over to the bar. Al picks up the stools.

SHEA
Should I call the police?

AL
No, no. This is my long time patron and ever other night he causes a scene.

Don plops down in a seat at the bar.

DON
I keep him good and on his toes.

SHEA
Isn't there a less expensive way to come in and say hello?

DON
Kids these days.

Don taps on the bar with his hand.

DON (CONT'D)
The usual Al.

Lux helps Al bring over a stool and put it back.

AL
It's going to be a sec.

Lux sits next to Don, Shea keeps his distance.

DON
You are definitely the cutest thing to come in the doors in quite some time. Must be my lucky day.

LUX
Or mine.

DON
I like her Al, get her a shot on my tab.

AL
You haven't paid your tab since 1983.

DON
This is true, but can you imagine when I do pay it? I'll own this place.

LUX
Not sure if that is how it works?

Shea begins to walk to the door.

AL
Sneaking out?

SHEA
Yeah, I think I'm going to call it a night.

LUX
What about a coffee?

SHEA
Nah, I should really get back.

Lux walks over to Shea and they are far enough away where their conversation can't be heard by the others.

LUX
So you've already established we aren't going to exchange numbers or see each other past tonight, I guess this is goodbye and be well.

SHEA
I guess so. Thank you for the company and conversation.

LUX
Likewise.

Shea and Lux look at each other awkwardly.

LUX (CONT'D)
Do we hug or something now?

Shea holds out his hand. Lux shakes his hand.

SHEA
Nice to meet you Lux with no story, destination, or current occupation.

LUX
Goodbye Shea, future man of many to be trapped in vows and always come in second at pool.

SHEA
Ouch.

Shea and Lux have a long last stare at each other.

Shea leaves. Lux goes back to the bar.

DON
Take it he wasn't your boyfriend?

LUX
Nope, I don't really have many of those.

DON
Shame.

LUX
Where's that drink you were going to buy me?

INT. THE POST - LATER

Don sleeps on the end of the bar. Al does a crossword as Lux builds something out of bar coasters.

Shea comes back in the bar. Don briefly wakes up and holds up his glass then lays back down. Al and Lux look at Shea.

LUX
Well, well. Did you pull a U-turn and come back?

Shea makes his way to the bar.

SHEA
I never left.

LUX
It's been almost an hour!

SHEA
My car wouldn't start, I left my lights on.

LUX
I could have given you a jump.

SHEA
I debated that.

Al slides a beer Shea's way.

AL
On the house.

LUX
So you've just been sitting outside this whole time?

SHEA
We had a good goodbye, I debated just calling a tow-

LUX
We did have a good adieu, but doesn't mean we couldn't have another.

SHEA
I didn't want you thinking I was coming back-

LUX
For me.

SHEA
Are you-

LUX
Going to finish all of your sentences?

SHEA
(Laughs)
Yeah.

LUX
Only until you stop trying to justify why you are in a chair next to me again.

SHEA
Fair enough.

LUX
But that was a good goodbye wasn't it?

SHEA
Totally, probably the easiest and most meaningful one I've ever had without trying. Why is that?

LUX
It's easy to say what we want to say when we know there is nothing to lose, no one to offend, or no chances being taken.

SHEA
I can agree with that.

Lux holds up her drink to his.

LUX
Cheers.

They cheers then take a drink.

LONG PAUSE.

SHEA
So be honest with me now, how are you here? Or more so, where are you on your way to or from?

LONG PAUSE as if Lux is in personal debate to answer.

LUX
My son died and I ran away from everything and everyone. My father had a lot of money and when he passed a few years back he left it all to me. I have no more family, no money troubles, and I'm just driving. Before my son's accident, I worked at a high school and taught the after school arts program.

SHEA
Husband?

LUX
Passed before our son was born.

Shea is in shock.

SHEA
I'm so sorry.

LUX
And I'm tired of people telling me that they are sorry, which is why I keep it to myself.

SHEA
(Waves at Al)
Can we get four shots of vodka?

AL
Well, definitely taking your keys now.

LUX
Are there cabs around here?

AL
Nope, but I do have a few rooms out back that I rent out from time to time and it's where him and I sleep.

All look down at Don who sleeps and SNORES.

AL (CONT'D)
Or I just leave him in here.

LUX
Is this like that one movie where you watch us from a hole in the wall, or chop us up?

AL
No, a little less dull than that. Just beds, toilet, small stand up shower, and the lucky one of you two gets a twelve inch black and white tv that, on most days, gets a few stations.

LUX
Dibs!

SHEA
Like I was going to win that.

Al serves their shots and walks away.

Shea pulls out a lighter.

SHEA (CONT'D)
I've only done this one other time.

LUX
Done what?

SHEA
After I light them, take the shot really quickly.

LUX
I am not doing that. I'll blow mine out first.

SHEA
No, no, come on. I promise, it gives it a fun taste.

LUX
A fun taste?

SHEA
Yeah, like dessert, but for adult consumption.

LUX
Hey Al, Shea is going to set the drinks on fire, is that ok with you?

Al just shrugs his shoulders and goes about what he was doing.

SHEA
On the count of three.

LUX
No, no, no-

Shea just stares at Lux.

LUX (CONT'D)
Ok, fine. One, two-

Shea lights the drinks.

SHEA
Cheers.

They quickly do their shots.

LUX
It does taste like an adult dessert, but I can't figure out like what though.

SHEA
Right? I've never had one that tasted like another.

LUX
So was there at reason you wanted to go with fire shots?

SHEA
I'm really bad at comfort and situational lulls.

LUX
I don't need you to be comforting.

SHEA
I know you don't, but me not trying to be comforting causes me to be comforting and when I'm suppose to be comforting I'm usually a complete ass. It has caused many of fights with my girlfriend.

LUX
Fiancee?

SHEA
(nods his head)
Fiancee.

LUX
Wow, you really don't like that word do you?

SHEA
I have no feelings on it one way or another. (Pause) Do you mind me asking what happened to your son?

LUX
He was on a class field trip to a farm. I was suppose to be one of the chaperones, but there was a last minute issue with the backdrop to the school play on opening night. I had to go across town to pick up a new black canvas because the other one was somehow torn with the school flag team was practicing in the auditorium. There were three or four other moms going on the field trip already, so me not going didn't seem like a big deal in the scheme of things. He was so excited to go.

SHEA
What was his name?

LUX
John, but everyone called him Johnny. He loved animals and petting them and he was so excited to see cow and horse poop for the first time because one of his friends told him how big the piles were.

Both LAUGH.

LUX (CONT'D)
I mean, excited. He talked about cow patties and horse turds for two weeks leading up to the trip. I stopped him at first and at the dinner table, but his general excitement kind of got me excited
(MORE)

LUX (CONT'D)
for him. I was going to Google it for him just so he could see a picture, but he wouldn't let me - he wanted his first time seeing it to be the real thing.

Lux's smile fades from her face.

LUX (CONT'D)
Johnny and a group of boys were flying kites in the field. One of the kites drifted over to the barn and he ran over to get it. Johnny was really good at climbing, and the kite was on the corner of the roof. He climbed up to get it.

SHEA
He fell?

LUX
He didn't fall, he actually got the kite down, and I guess curiosity got the best of him or he heard the horses because he went in the barn where the horses were. Not only did he go in the barn, he went into one of the stalls where the horse was, I suspect it was to see the poop. The stall he went into was a sick horse who had been aggressive recently while getting treatment for something or another. No one knows the exact details, but I feel like he wanted to get close to see the large pile of poop and he got too close to the horse, the horse kicked Johnny in the head. Johnny died instantly.

Shea can't think of anything to say.

LUX (CONT'D)
I play that over and over in my head. And the odds of that happening are so low that no online search could provide an answer because of it's rarity. In a blink I lost my whole life.

Lux takes a long drink.

SHEA

I'm so sorry. I know you probably don't want to hear that, or you're tired of hearing that, but the random circumstances of that situation warrants a genuine apology from the Universe for the components of that happening.

LUX

Well, that apology I will accept.

SHEA

Do you have friends where you are from?

LUX

Of course I have friends.

SHEA

No, I don't mean it like that. Like, did you say goodbye to anyone, or did you just leave?

LUX

I just left. The people who knew me understand why. Everyone else, it doesn't really matter.

Shea nods his head.

LUX (CONT'D)

Well, now that I was just a mood killer, how about we look into getting some food?

SHEA

You aren't a mood killer, thank you for sharing. I know that couldn't be easy.

LUX

It still doesn't feel real. But really - food, come on.

SHEA

I don't think Al has a menu.

LUX

Al!

Al walks up.

AL
More shots again?

LUX
Not this round. How does food delivery look around here?

AL
Not great. But I have mini-frozen pizzas, pizza rolls, and pizza bagels.

SHEA
Anything not pizza related?

AL
I can take the pizza toppings off the bagels and there would be just bagels.

LUX
I'll take a mini-pizza.

SHEA
I'll have what the lady is having.

AL
Give me seven minutes and forty seconds for the both of them.

LUX
Nice to see that you have it down to a science.

EXT. THE POST - LATER

Shea and Lux eat pizza by the fire. Shea flips through pictures on his phone.

SHEA
Here's a good one.

Shea shows Lux the picture.

LUX
Aw, how adorable.

SHEA
I am such a sucker for cats. If I could have a house with rooms of cats I totally would.

LUX
Are you serious? You wouldn't be able to co-inhabit a place like that.

SHEA
It would be big enough.

LUX
What, like ten or fifteen cats?

SHEA
Thirty plus.

LUX
Oh my goodness, you are crazy!

SHEA
Tammy is allergic in general though, so we can't even get one. She wants a reptile or a spider.

LUX
I'm sorry, is your soon to be wife's name, Tammy?

Lux LAUGHS.

SHEA
Oh come on, and Lux, what kind of name is that.

LUX
Oh, my name is awesome. Tammy is like a suburban house wife from the 70s or 80s with a large poof on her head.

SHEA
It was her mom's name and for some reason her mom named her Tammy Jr.

Lux about falls over with LAUGHTER.

LUX
That makes it so much worse.

SHEA
Alright, alright.

LUX
Shea and Tammy. Is there going to be a Tammy the 3rd running around in your future?

SHEA
Man, you really are enjoying yourself aren't you?

LUX
I am, thank you.

SHEA
I feel like I should abruptly change the subject to religion or politics.

LUX
Are you going into politics?

SHEA
No, not really into the different parties and lying or sucking up to people for votes.

LUX
That's a shame, Tammy would make a great name for a politician's wife!

Shea leans back in his chair unamused.

LUX (CONT'D)
Ok, ok, that was my last one, at least for now. I promise.

SHEA
For real promise?

LUX
I for real promise.

SHEA
So religion it is.

LUX
Golden Boy goes first.

SHEA
I was raised Lutheran, but my fiancee has us go to a Catholic church.

LUX
That, for me, is a really tough sell.

SHEA
Well what do you believe in, if anything?

LUX
I believe in the wonderful infinite.

SHEA
What does that mean?

LUX
Textbook, or Bible wise, religions are great for teaching morals, keeping some followers in-line, giving hope - but aside from all of that, there is so much more. There are the unseen feelings, flows of motion, and energy pocket that makes us all just dominoes waiting to be tipped over, or tip someone else over in a long string of uncontrollable events just to be stood back up for it all to happen again.

SHEA
I do like dominoes.

LUX
Yeah, they are pretty cool. I enjoy them when I am not being lined up like one.

SHEA
So what is the wonderful infinite?

LUX
The point beyond all of this.

SHEA
A little vague for such a bold concept.

LUX
Well that is just the premise. Take what you want from it.

SHEA
What do you take from it, or at least why do you believe in that?

LUX
After a long day, or even my son's death- there is always a moment.
(MORE)

LUX (CONT'D)
Even if in it's most brief of time, where there is a pause of existence. The moment is a glimpse from the infinite and a reminder that now means nothing in the entirety of life.

SHEA
A little bland or at least a sad way to look at life, don't you think?

LUX
It's not suppose to be a sad or bland thing, actually hopeful. If there is nothing and when our almighty aging sun dies out, all life will die out with it.

SHEA
That's only if our homes on Mars don't work out.

LUX
Same solar system genius. Anyway, Knowing that the world is on its way to being nothing, makes me recognize the something that we are. It's not a religion or anything thing to follow or live by, I just believe in the infinite that will surpass time itself.

SHEA
You do know there are other things to believe in before the lights turn out?

LUX
Yeah, but I don't support something that creates so much war, where is the peace and divine serenity in that?

SHEA
I get what you are saying, I just don't have a response.

LUX
Too much?

SHEA
Not at all. I guess my mind currently doesn't expand that far.

SHEA (CONT'D)
We should go back to talking about pets.

LUX
Or your wedding.

SHEA
Really?

LUX
Why not?

SHEA
No reason, sure, let's talk about it.

LUX
Top three reasons she is the one you want to spend the rest of your life with?

SHEA
Wow, how long have you been waiting to blurt that one out?

LUX
Don't change the subject.

Shea pauses to think.

SHEA
She gets my sense of humor.

LUX
That's easy to do, you're not that funny.

SHEA
(Gives Lux a look)
Two, my parents love her.

LUX
That's not a reason why you want to spend your life with someone.

SHEA
My parents are very particular and if she can tame them and their absurd expectations and
(MORE)

SHEA (CONT'D)
questioning, she has a quality that I love.

LUX
Fine, but the last reason better be a lot better then the first two.

Shea thinks for a moment.

SHEA
I genuinely enjoy waking up to her every day.

LUX
That is a good one.

SHEA
There you go.

LUX
Ok, ok, what about three reasons you don't want to spend the rest of your life with her?

Shea goes to speak but Lux stops him.

LUX (CONT'D)
Nope, just think about it for a minute.

Shea sits there for a few seconds and stares at the fire.

SHEA
No, I really don't have a an answer, or three. I guess I may not have the strongest feelings about marriage, but it has nothing to do with me not wanting to be with her.

Lux, for the first time, has no response.

Shea and Lux sit back in their chairs and watch the fire.

INT. THE POST - LATER THAT NIGHT

Al watches television. Shea comes in.

AL
Haven't seen you guys in awhile, was about to head out and check on you after my show.

SHEA
Yeah, we're still out there.

AL
She seems like a sweet girl.

SHEA
She is.

AL
Are y'all getting two rooms or one?

SHEA
Two. It's not that kind of hang out.

AL
Yeah, it doesn't seem like it, but it's not my place to judge neither.

SHEA
She is something special though.

AL
She also got you to stay for one more drink.

SHEA
That she did. Speaking of, can we have one last round and then can we maybe get the keys to the rooms?

AL
Drinks, coming right up. And no need for keys, all of the rooms are unlocked except for mine.

SHEA
A little unsafe out in the middle of nowhere don't you think?

AL
I double lock the bar and there is no way back to the rooms. I have no interest in watching you sleep, it's all safe.

SHEA
(Shea nods towards Don)
What about-

AL
Harmless, plus he usually stays in the room with me.

SHEA
Oh.

AL
Problem with that?

SHEA
Not at all.

Al slides Shea drinks.

AL
I'll be around for about another half hour if you change your mind or need anything.

EXT. THE POST - PATIO - MINUTES LATER

Shea delivers a drink to Lux.

SHEA
You ready to stand up a minute?

LUX
Maybe, why? Another bar fight or something?

SHEA
The rooms are unlocked- I'm dying to see what they look like.

LUX
Where are they even at?

SHEA
I guess straight back. Al said they aren't locked.

LUX
What about that other guy in there?

SHEA
He stays in Al's room I just found out.

LUX
Aw, good for Al.

Shea and Lux head off towards the back.

EXT. BEHIND THE POST - MINUTES LATER

A small motel can be seen after Lux and Shea emerge from the woods. The motel is run down, chip painted, no sign, looks abandoned or like it could be a small apartment complex.

LUX
I swear they've made a movie that started out exactly like this.

SHEA
Yeah, I'm a little inclined to sleep in my car.

LUX
It can't be that bad, Al lives here.

SHEA
That means nothing.

LUX
What if there are water beds inside!

SHEA
An even bigger sign to not go in.

Lux walks towards the motel.

SHEA (CONT'D)
I could just call a cab.

LUX
You could. And go back to the hotel and life will go on just as it was. Ooooooor, you could see what is behind door number 2, literally.

Lux points to the door where a number 2 hangs.

Shea thinks for a moment and then walks towards the motel.

SHEA
Curiosity does have the best of me right now.

LUX
That's the spirit.

INT. ROOM 2 - MOMENTS LATER

The room has one large twin bed, a side table with a lamp, and a 12 inch tv on a small dresser stand. Plain walls except for one wall has a very small picture of a fish that hangs off center. There is a single chair in the corner of the room.

The door slowly opens, and then it swings all the way open. Shea and Lux stand in the doorway.

LUX
Definitely made for simple living.

Lux walks in first.

LUX (CONT'D)
Yes, the one with the tv. I guess this is my suite.

SHEA
No water bed, it's probably in my room.

Lux bounces on the bed and quickly stops.

LUX
This is what it is like to bounce on a rock. I think I just hurt my spine.

Shea sits in the chair.

SHEA
Not too bad. Nice and stiff, probably great for posture and back support.

LUX
The tv has a knob, now that is cute. So when's the last time you brought a girl to a motel room that wasn't your fiance?

Shea is completely caught off guard.

SHEA
I'm going to be sleeping in the other room.

LUX
Relax, I know. I was just messing with you and asking a question, not trying to hit a nerve.

SHEA
No, I just don't want to give the wrong impression.

LUX
There is no idea to give.

SHEA
I know, I just feel like I'm doing something wrong.

LUX
Why is that?

SHEA
I don't know. I can't remember the last time my fiancee and I just talked, let alone the whole night. And I've spent the whole night seamlessly able to hang out and talk with you.

LUX
Yeah, but you know your wife and there are less things to ask about.

SHEA
Should it be that way though? Are we going to eventually run out of things to talk about and my life is weekend brunches with my parents just to spark an alternative conversation?

LUX
Do you guys plan on having kids? I hear they are great distractions for relationships.

SHEA
She wants three, I could settle on two. But I still want to be able to talk with her, and have a night where we get an overnight baby sitter so we go out and drink all night. We would talk about our first date, then I give her my coat as we walk in the moonlight night not even caring about the time. I imagine that happening, I want that to happen, but then I blink and reality sets in. I fear we just end up at a hotel where she passes out at eight and I'm
(MORE)

SHEA (CONT'D)
left watching porn that does nothing for me because I feel bad for the girls in the video and wonder where their parents are to get them out of whatever situation got them into porn in the first place.

LUX
(Joking)
So you have some worry.

SHEA
It's normal though, who doesn't worry about life changing decisions?

LUX
While it is good to plan ahead with some things, you have to remember to not get ahead of the now. You are already driving a minivan-

SHEA
She promised no minivans, but what if they are more economical and-

Shea stops himself to let Lux finish.

LUX
Thank you. You are ten years ahead of one day from now, just like you were earlier. Don't let what's happening in front of you get ruined because there is no guarantee for how it will turn out, or because there's no instruction manual.

SHEA
I know, I just don't know how to not think beyond today or even this week.

LUX
If you are with the right person, then you shouldn't have to worry about having all the answers. The nice part about being with someone you love is that they help you figure out every question that comes your way. Your worries are their worries, your walls are
(MORE)

LUX (CONT'D)
their walls. Is Tammy (laughs)... sorry, Tammy, still gets me. Is your fiancee good at finding answers with you?

SHEA
Nothing really major has come up, I'm sure she would be though.

LUX
What about your wedding? That seems a little major to me.

SHEA
She's planned everything, all I had to do was attend tastings and pick out my suit. I guess she is really good about organizing and making sure all is taken care of. She even made sure I was happy with her decisions.

LUX
There you go.

SHEA
Yeah, I guess I really haven't thought about a lot of things, I've just been worrying about them. Your husband, did you know he was the one?

LUX
From the moment I first saw his piercing blue eyes, there were no doubts. But not everyone gets that magical moment, they should, but all love is different and so is the magic that makes it so wonderful.

SHEA
Do you think you will ever fall in love again, or have another kid?

LUX
I am in the now, I'm nowhere near years from now.

SHEA
You are just doing what you are doing?

LUX
Going to drive until I hit a coast, then maybe turn around and do it again on a different route.

SHEA
Sounds like it will get lonely?

LUX
Not if I keep meeting people like you.

SHEA
I'm one of a kind. You won't find me in other states.

Lux and Shea share a smile that lasts a second too long.

LUX
Alright, back to one night stands, how many have you had?

SHEA
You do not stop until your questions get answered, do you?

LUX
Nope, plus, consider this your last confession as a single guy. Marriage is where all secrets go to die.

SHEA
That's so sad, no.

LUX
Yup, that I Do is a soft goodbye to all secrets to yourself.

SHEA
First, I have never had a one night stand.

LUX
Never? Alright, a little surprised, but I like it. Second?

SHEA
Second, people are allowed to have secrets even when they are married.

LUX
No they aren't, they so aren't.

SHEA
People are still individuals even when they get married. You don't give up your personal thoughts or other private things in marriage.

LUX
Private things? Like what? If you are talking about sex with yourself, believe me, she knows.

SHEA
No, not that, like collecting stamps or chatting online with a priest.

Lux LAUGHS.

LUX
I don't even know how to respond to that. How often are you messaging your minister and why?

SHEA
That was just an example.

LUX
An awful example. And collecting stamps, is that just a secret because it's embarrassing?

SHEA
Maybe not the best example, but you get what I am saying.

LUX
Face it, there are no secrests without shame. And unless you clear your browser history every time you use it, your private online chats are up for grabs as well. A marriage is a contract to be a duo for eternity. What is the big deal anyway? You should be able to share everything with your best friend.

SHEA
I never said she was my best friend, I mean she is, but that is a cheesy way to look at it.

LUX
Everyone sees it differently.

SHEA
Yup.

There is a lull.

LUX
So.

SHEA
So.

LUX
Tired at all?

SHEA
You would think after talking with you all night I would be, but surprisingly, I am not.

LUX
What is that supposed to mean?

SHEA
I was kidding.

LUX
You're a little exhausting yourself.

SHEA
Maybe I should head over to my room.

LUX
Yeah. Or! OR! One last game of pool and line of shots.

SHEA
Excuse me, line of shots?

LUX
Before I never see you again, I have a few more blunt questions for you, Shot per question, no explanations, no stories, just the honest truth.

Shea thinks for a moment.

SHEA
Let's do it.

INT. THE POST - POOL TABLE - MINUTES LATER

Lux racks the pool balls as Shea picks out a pool cue. Al comes over with a drink in his hand, he takes a sip.

AL
I thought you guys were calling it a night?

LUX
Almost, got one last spurt in us. Can we get a bottle of whiskey and a couple shot glasses?

AL
Going to pour them yourselves now?

LUX
Yeah, if that's ok?

AL
Oh, what the hell, why not? Did you have a chance to check out the rooms yet?

SHEA
We did. They are simple.

AL
I don't crowd the rooms with a bunch of unnecessary things, I keep them practical.

LUX
It's nice to have a place to stay, thank you.

AL
Sometimes a good bed with a fluffy pillow can make all the difference. No need for wifi and minibars.

SHEA
Plus, who needs a minibar when there is a full bar only a walk away?

AL
I think you are missing the point.

LUX
I think he was just kidding.

AL
Joke or not, the simple things get overshadowed way too often by conglomerate merchandising and everyone needing everything one second faster then they did the way before. When I was your age we called people on the telephone and took the time to handwrite letters. Now, everyone just texts because they can't be bothered to even speak to the person they want to talk with. I just don't get it.

LUX
Different generations and expectations.

AL
Your generation seems to try to make things easier for themselves, but really all electronics have done is burn holes in pockets and cut out the beautiful essence in life of talking with people. One reason I love owning this bar is because I get to watch people talk, like you two for example, no phones in your hands, no flat screen computers, just good old fashion conversation. It's a beautiful thing that I hope doesn't die.

LUX
The one flaw with time is that everything eventually dies.

AL
The truth. That is all too true.

SHEA
Well, we appreciate your bar and what you've got going on here.

AL
Appreciation is also a gesture going out the with the changing decades.

Al walks away but continues to talk.

AL (CONT'D)
Would it kill a twenty one year old to say please or thank you?
(MORE)

AL (CONT'D)
It's just the thought of the matter.

Lux and Shea share a small LAUGH.

SHEA
He totally reminds me of my grandpa.

LUX
So cute.

SHEA
Are we going to do this?

LUX
Yes, there are still a few things I want to know about my friend Shea before the morning light intros our goodbyes and you become just a faint memory in my life timeline.

SHEA
Maybe we could write letters to each other, that would make Al really happy.

LUX
I don't know. Have you ever just needed a night where you could let it all out with no repercussions the next day? That's how I feel tonight.

SHEA
Everything in a sense has repercussions. Without a doubt I am going to hear about this tomorrow, but I really don't care. Single-handedly it seems that you have made the concept of care go out the window.

LUX
Is that a good thing or bad?

SHEA
It's just a thing and there is nothing good or bad about it. Like if I blink tomorrow, I will feel like none of this was even real, which is fine to an extent, but in so many ways all I want is this
(MORE)

SHEA (CONT'D)
night to be real for days to come, and maybe even longer.

LUX
Shea, I can't-

SHEA
No, not in the scheme that I want it to be you and I. But more that I just want to be able to speak without doubt, or wishing that I voiced other words or thoughts. Tammy is great and I really can talk with her, but it really comes down to the fact that I worry about what I have evolved into, and if my words will match who I was years ago. Will I still be the same person she wanted years from now?

LUX
Personally, I hope not. If this is you evolved, who will you be when another revolution of yourself comes around?

SHEA
Easier said as an idea.

LUX
True, but let me then ask, has she evolved or even made strides in advancement since you have or at least since you have been together? Or is she still the same person?

Shea takes a second to think. Shea prepares to "break" the pool balls.

SHEA
Staying who you are isn't a bad thing, I mean, isn't that the person I feel in love with?

LUX
I'm going to overstep again- is it you, or you from years ago that fell in love with her? And now you feel obligated to follow that up with a commitment?

Shea is in deep internal debate, but it is broken up when Al walks up with a bottle of whiskey and three shot glasses.

AL
On the house, as long as the first round is with me.

Lux puts her arm around Al.

LUX
I think we can reach a bargain with your hard compromise.

Al opens the bottle and pours three shots.

AL
Why are you both even here?

LUX
We've talked it out, this or that is what it comes down to.

AL
Not good enough for me. If I am going to cheers, it's only fair I know how you arrived here in the first place. It is no secret that our bar is off the beaten path. SOOOO, when a couple of straight shooters arrive with no backstory and only orders one round, yet checks in for sun-up, I think as a person I can cheers to the fellow lost or at least guide you off this path.

SHEA
Al, you are something special.

AL
Hands off Tiger, you know that I am spoken for.

SHEA
Ha ha, come on.

Lux helps adds her charm.

LUX
Oh, I'd steal your heart in a rock water skip, if you were single. But, not really in the mood to shell out a detailed story, kind of already did that tonight.

Al and Shea stare for a second at Lux.

SHEA
Same page as her.

LUX
Nope, you can't cop out. Tell Al more about your upcoming nuptials.

SHEA
Na, I'm good. Plus, you have both already had your opinion how my feelings and future are about to play out, there is a deposit down and commitment made. I honor those things.

AL
Honor is not valor.

SHEA
What could you possibly know about that situation? What do you know about honor?

Al angrily drops the whiskey and his shot glass on the table, appears tipsy himself.

AL
Don't be pompous. Your kindness and candor has carried you this far. Not that it's any of your business, but decades before you were even conceived, I was defending the world that makes your life possible.

LUX
And a beautiful world it is.

SHEA
I wasn't disrespecting you, your time, or history- I just came here for a beer. No need for you to dive into my reasoning or intentions. There is no strategy. I don't want any conflict, I appreciate your service. Right now, it's just a late night and we're drinking, that's it.

Lux consoles Al.

LUX
Alright, this accelerated fast and out of nowhere. Al, we appreciate your bar and for letting us hang out, you've been a wonderful host. Shea is just being a little sensative right now.

Lux puts her arm around Al.

SHEA
Seemingly, you two are teaming up.

LUX
No, all is fine. Al here, he's a good guy with life experience. Could maybe even teach us a thig or two, right? Like about love- in just a few minutes with Don, you could tell he was happy.

Lux pours shots.

SHEA
You think that I can't have that?

LUX
It's hard to have an opinion when you have no feeling behind your thoughts.

Shea looks at Al. Al knows what Shea thinks.

AL
Before I loved that guy over there, I was married to a woman for seventeen years. Alice. I loved her with every breath. There was no blink of the eye where she was not the hope in my day and the sunset at the end of it.

Lux begins to tears up.

AL (CONT'D)
Love, like time, does not stop. I stopped being creepy and looking at her picture every day and having all of her stuff overwhelm my living space. But she is still in my every day in one way or another. While her knitted blankets, handmade crafts, family pictures, and relatives seeped out of my life over years - Alice, is
(MORE)

AL (CONT'D)
tattooed to my life, my soul, today, and tomorrow.

Al points to Don.

AL (CONT'D)
I know I love him, I also know that I am not taken away from my love for Alice. If someone loves you, like LOVES you without conditions or cause, then their love extends to your happiness and what it can be.

LUX
You are hitting close to home.

AL
Alright, let's pour these drinks.

Lux takes her time to rack the balls on the pool table.

Al holds up his shot.

AL (CONT'D)
Continuously, the world has only allowed me to gain from loss. You can make it to the end like that, but sometimes, we don't want to go any further. So we retire to the land of the lost and failed ambitions on the Island of Sad. Yet, we are all okay with it.

Lux takes a shot with Al, Shea walks off.

SHEA
I need to use the restroom.

LUX
Thank you Al. I think we are just going to finish up this game and crash for the night.

AL
The bottle is on the house. I'm going to lock the front and head to bed.

LUX
Good night.

AL
Night.

Al locks up, turns off the tv, grabs Don and then heads to bed. A few of the lights shut off, the only main lighting is over the pool area.

Lux goes and helps herself behind the bar and comes back with an armfull of shot glasses. She lines them up on the edge of a nearby table and fills each of them with shots, one by one. She empties the entire bottle of whiskey and then places it in the middle of the shots.

Lux chalks her pool cue.

Shea returns.

LUX
That was a long visit.

SHEA
I just needed a minute before coming back out. Did I miss close?

LUX
Al turned in for the night, but we still have a game and those.

Shea sees the long row of shots.

SHEA
Maybe we should call it as well?

LUX
Some buttons got pushed. What do you expect from complete strangers though?

SHEA
I was just expecting a beer.

LUX
And aren't you happy that you got so much more instead?

Shea finally cracks a smile. He walks over to the shots.

SHEA
This is it.

LUX
This is it.

Lux grabs a filled shot glass, Shea does the same.

LUX (CONT'D)
Democrat or Republican?

SHEA
(Laughs)
You are awful at this.

LUX
Don't change the subject.

SHEA
Republican.

LUX
I knew it!

SHEA
How could you know that?

LUX
There is an invisible patch on your sleeve that appears sometimes.

SHEA
What do you mean?

Lux shrugs, then takes her shot. Shea follows her lead and takes his shot.

LUX
What about female republicans?

SHEA
What about?

LUX
I be okay with you being a Republican, but an anti-

SHEA
Yes, Republican females are fantastic. I can only guess your stance?

Lux returns to the pool table.

LUX
It may come to a surprise to you, but I don't really have a stance. Politics can be like infants that don't get their way, so it's hard to side one way or the other.

Lux makes a shot.

SHEA
Is it even your turn?

LUX
Sure. Let's just take turns.

SHEA
That is not how the game goes.

Shea takes the pool cue and sets up to shoot.

SHEA (CONT'D)
And no, I am not surprised by that answer. Well, I was going to guess liberal, but your response is just the same.

LUX
Not the same at all.

SHEA
Honestly, I haven't voted in the last two elections. I really don't put much stock in the notion that any person should have a say in how others live their lives.

Shea makes a shot and sets up for another.

LUX
Well, if people like you, who adopt a political label don't care- then what chance do people like me have, who take no oppositional stand either way? Who's really running this joint?

Shea makes another shot.

SHEA
Yet another open-ended question.

Shea grabs a shot from the table. Lux joins him.

LUX
Your question, make it good.

SHEA
My questions are always good.

LUX
So far.

Shea thinks for a second.

SHEA
Are you afraid of roller coasters?

LUX
Really? You are sometimes more random than I give you credit for.

SHEA
I just like me some coasters.

Shea takes his shot, Lux follows.

LUX
Depends on their age. Like if they are wooden, or the newer steel and fiberglass models. The old, wooden ones are really rickety.

SHEA
Yeah, but those are the good ones! Those are the ones where you really feel like you don't know if you are going to live, or die, or fly off into the crowd below.

LUX
That's the real appeal though, isn't it? Roller coasters aren't the tea cup rides.

SHEA
Not that there is anything wrong with the tea cups, but things like that are just rides, they aren't coasters. Tea cups are a whole different type of question and conversation.

Shea returns to the pool table.

LUX
Isn't it my go?

SHEA
I am playing by pool rules, not "every other shot, made up" rules.

LUX
Fine, fine. Well, overall, I do like roller coasters and their brief mini rushes, but the hour lines to actually get to the sixty
(MORE)

LUX (CONT'D)
second spin and turn really makes the experience not worth it.

Shea makes another shot.

SHEA
That is just all a part of the anticipation and what makes the ride even better.

LUX
I don't like waiting, which is probably why I like the tea cups and rides like it. There are barely, if ever, any other riders. I can hop off an hop right back on if I want.

SHEA
But there is value in the wait.

LUX
Not always.

SHEA
Can you agree it's worth taking the chance though?

LUX
What, take a chance on waiting for something that may disappoint or may satisfy while spending longer in the wait then in the actual moment?

Shea misses his shot and gives Lux the pool cue.

SHEA
Yeah, I guess. Not everything should be an instant gratification.

LUX
Good things shouldn't always require a wait.

Shea and Lux are caught in a stare.

SHEA
You're up.

LUX
I know I am. I'm just trying to think of a middle ground to all of this.

Shea shrugs.

LUX (CONT'D)
You can't shrug, that's my thing.

Lux sets up to take a shot.

SHEA
What about the rides with water, like the log thing. It takes a few minutes to climb up and that is where the anticipation starts and then in seconds you crash down into the water?

LUX
That is somewhat of a middle ground.

Lux makes the shot.

LUX (CONT'D)
I'm doing awesome.

SHEA
Very proud of yourself, aren't you?

LUX
I just like winning, or at least getting in more balls then you.

SHEA
Isn't that the same thing?

LUX
Kind Of.

Shea grabs two shots and passes one to Lux.

SHEA
Here, this will help get more balls in.

LUX
Circumcision!

SHEA
(laughs)
What?

LUX
That is going to be my next question, I just didn't want to forget.

Lux takes her shot. Shea takes his.

SHEA
How is that even a question?

LUX
Like, what do you think of it? Is it a cosmetic choice, or a necessity?

SHEA
It's just a must. You aren't a good parent unless you do. Boys who don't just get laughed at in the locker room and turned down by girls.

LUX
I don't believe that, I would never turn down a guy because of that.

SHEA
Have you seen what it looks like on a grown man?

LUX
Well no, but it can't be that bad.

SHEA
No, it's just why you can say you wouldn't turn a guy down because of it.

Lux sets up for another shot.

LUX
Oh whatever, I'll look it up on the Internet.

SHEA
I wouldn't do that, you know what kind of pictures would pop up?

Lux accidentally knocks in the 8-ball.

SHEA (CONT'D)
You just lost!

LUX
No I didn't, I'm solids!

SHEA
That was the black ball.

LUX
That was the purple one.

Shea grabs the purple solid ball and holds it up.

SHEA
This is the purple ball.

Lux tries to grab the ball and wrestles with Shea. Lux is in Shea's arms.

Shea kisses Lux. Lux firmly pushes Shea away.

LUX
What are you doing?

SHEA
I'm sorry, I just blinked and then didn't think.

LUX
You sure didn't. And in doing so, you've missed the whole point of this night.

SHEA
Which was what? Two strangers drinking at a dive bar?

LUX
Which was being attached without making an attachment.

SHEA
What? What are you even talking about?

LUX
You just don't get it. I feel sorry for your fiancee.

SHEA
Don't worry about her.

LUX
Someone should.

SHEA
What is that supposed to mean?

LUX
Nothing.

SHEA
No, what?

LUX
I'm going to bed. This night really is over now.

Lux walks away, Shea tries to grab her arm to stop her. Lux pulls away.

LUX (CONT'D)
Don't.

Shea lets her go. Lux leaves. Shea throws the purple pool ball.

Shea goes to the shots, takes a couple. After a pause, he knocks the rest of them off.

Shea closes his eyes for a moment. When he opens them, he leaves.

EXT. BEHIND THE POST - SUN UP

The sun just starts to come up. Al is outside, he paints the side of the motel.

Shea comes out from his room quietly and walks softly away.

AL
What, no goodbye?

Shea is briefly startled and looks at Lux's door to make sure she isn't there.

SHEA
Shhh.

AL
The old sneak off.

SHEA
It isn't like that.

AL
Alright.

SHEA
What are you doing up so early?

AL
I'm always up at this time. I like
to watch the sunrise. Do you need
a jump still?

SHEA
I was just going to call someone.

Al puts down his brush and wipes off his hands.

AL
No need, come on.

Shea follows Al.

EXT. THE POST PARKING LOT - MINUTES LATER

Al hooks up jumper cables from one car to another.

AL
It's been awhile since I've jumped
a car.

SHEA
Can't say that I ever have.

AL
Do you usually just call someone?

SHEA
Well, yeah, but that is what a car
maintenance plan is for.

AL
It's a dieing generation of doing
things for yourself.

SHEA
I can do things for myself.

AL
Where does the black handle go and
where does the red one go?

Shea thinks for a minute.

SHEA
Trick question, because it doesn't matter.

AL
Thank the stars you aren't doing this right now, you'd be blown to Timbuktu.

SHEA
Ok, I get it. Thank you for your help.

Al attaches the cables then starts his car.

AL
We just have to wait about fifteen minutes, and then you can be on your way. Want a cup of coffee while you wait?

SHEA
That would be fantastic.

Al leaves. Shea sits on the ground and leans against the building. He closes his eyes.

LUX
You were sneaking out too, huh?

Shea opens his eyes and sees Lux.

SHEA
I just wanted to get back.

LUX
I get it.

Shea goes to stand but Lux stops him and sits.

LUX (CONT'D)
No need, Al is making coffee, may be a minute.

They sit in silence for a second.

SHEA
I want to apologize. I feel like I ruined the whole night and it was a mistake.

LUX
It was a mistake, but you didn't ruin the whole night. We should have just gone to bed, but
(MORE)

LUX (CONT'D)
something in both of us wanted to stay up.

SHEA
The booze?

LUX
Probably. That, and we connected. Sometimes that just feels good and people over embrace it to a point where they cross a line of regret.

SHEA
I don't regret the night.

LUX
I don't either. I think we came to the line, put a foot over, and then stopped.

Shea nods.

SHEA
So what now? Are we still saying our goodbyes and then part ways for good?

LUX
(Nods)
Yup.

SHEA
That's what we talked about, it's probably best.

LUX
I wouldn't crash your wedding.

SHEA
I don't think you would. But what if in a year or so from now I get in a fight with my wife and seek comfort else where, turn to you, and then cross that line of no return?

LUX
Who is to say I would let you?

SHEA
It's about the fact that I would doubt myself and I don't want to
(MORE)

SHEA (CONT'D)
doubt myself. Not that I do, but none of us know our future selves.

LUX
I get it. Perhaps we will meet again in a dive bar down the road in a state we've only ventured to that one time, and across the room- boom, we air cheers and a conversation will inevitably strike up.

SHEA
Is that an optimistic thought, or just part of the goodbye?

LUX
A little of both.

SHEA
We could always do that thing, meet here in one year-

LUX
No, we can't. One, it is cliche.

SHEA
And two?

LUX
We should never have relationships in our lives that may affect or upset our significant others.

SHEA
Alright.

Shea and Lux lean against the wall in silence.

MOMENTS LATER.

LUX
I'm glad you didn't just leave.

SHEA
I feel like Al had something to do with that.

LUX
Probably.

SHEA
Man, I am hungover.

LUX
Yeah, I have to go get some greasy bacon somewhere.

SHEA
And a Bloody Mary.

LUX
Oh, I don't know about that. I could go either way. One would make me feel better, the other would leave me embarrassed from vomiting in public.

SHEA
Probably shouldn't then, to be on the safe side.

LUX
Probably not.

Al returns with two cups of coffee.

AL
Is black alright?

LUX
It's coffee, that's all I care about right now.

Al walks over to the car to check on it.

AL
Should be ready soon. Do you want to try and start 'er up?

Shea starts his car.

AL (CONT'D)
You look good to go. Just let it run for a short while and you can be on your way.

The sun is almost completely up. Al unhooks the jumper cables.

Shea gets out of his car and shakes Al's hand.

SHEA
Thanks for everything. No hard feelings for late last night I hope?

AL
You were nothing. I get some strange folks off the main road and I've had to kick many out. Safe travels and may the road take you where you need to be.

Shea smiles and nods his head.

AL (CONT'D)
Well, I'll leave you two to it. Don't be a stranger in these parts and you both always have a shot waiting if you find your way back here.

Lux gives Al a hug which he halfway returns and then leaves.

Lux and Shea slowly walk towards each other, they drink their coffee.

LUX
Any big plans for the day?

SHEA
Oh, you know, just entertaining a couple hundred people and being agreeable. You?

LUX
The open road.

SHEA
Any thoughts on where you are heading to next?

LUX
I'm going to run out the tank of gas I have now, fill it up again and then see how far that takes me.

SHEA
Is your last stop going to be a bar?

LUX
Jealous I may meet someone like you, making you just another guy along the road in my travels?

SHEA
It did cross my mind in a weird way.

LUX
Why in a weird way?

SHEA
I've never stayed up all night at a bar, nor just talked with someone. I don't know-

LUX
No, I get it. It's an unduplicable rarity.

SHEA
(Smiles)
Unduplicable rarity.

Lux holds out her coffee mug to cheers, Shea responds.

Shea and Lux watch the sunrise together.

LUX (V.O.)
It was a moment that lasted from dusk till dawn, it was a moment unlike any other, and then it was over in a blink.

MINUTES LATER

At sun up, Lux and Shea hug then get in their cars.

EXT. THE POST PARKING LOT - MINUTES LATER

Shea drives one way out of the lot, Lux drives the opposite direction.

ONE YEAR LATER

INT. THE POST - NIGHT

Al and Don watch tv. DOOR OPENS behind them. Al turns to greet the person who cannot be seen on camera.

AL
Well look who it is.

Al pores a shot and slides it on the bar.

AL (CONT'D)
As promised if you ever were to return.

All that can be seen is an undefined arm raise the shot.

AL (CONT'D)
Cheers.

FADE OUT.

www.ingramcontent.com/pod-product-compliance
Lightning Source LLC
LaVergne TN
LVHW010457160826
845677LV00012B/2519